CLAUDIA

CAST OF

CLAUDIA

That's me. I'm thirteen, and I'm in the seventh grade at Pine Tree Middle School. I live with my mom, my dad, and my brother, Jimmy. I have one cat, Ping-Ping. I like music, baseball, and hanging out with my friends.

ME

MONICA is my very best friend. We met when we were really little, and we've been best friends ever since. I don't know what I'd do without her! Monica loves horses. In fact, when she grows up, she wants to be an Olympic rider!

MONICA

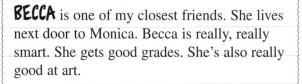

BECCA is one of my closest friends. She lives next door to Monica. Becca is really, really smart. She gets good grades. She's also really good at art.

BECCA

CHARACTERS

TOMMY's our class clown. Sometimes he's really funny, but sometimes he is just annoying. Becca has a crush on him . . . but I'd never tell.

TOMMY

PETER

I think **PETER** is probably the smartest person I've ever met. Seriously. He's even smarter than our teachers! He's also one of my friends. Which is lucky, because sometimes he helps me with homework.

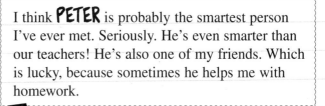

ADAM and I met when we were in third grade. Now that we're teenagers, we don't spend as much time together as we did when we were kids, but he's always there for me when I need him. (Plus, he's the only person who wants to talk about baseball with me!)

ADAM

CAST OF

BRAD TURINO is the guy I like at school. He's so cute! He's a star on the football team, and he's also a really, really nice guy.

BRAD

JIMMY is my big brother. He's obsessed with video games and computers. He doesn't talk to me very much, except when I do something to annoy him. I usually try to stay out of his way, but sometimes he helps me out.

JIMMY

NICK is my annoying seven-year-old neighbor. I get stuck babysitting him a lot. He likes to make me miserable. (Okay, he's not that bad ALL of the time . . . just most of the time.)

NICK

CHARACTERS

MR. AND MRS. GOMEZ are my neighbors. Even though they are old enough to be my grandparents, I consider them my good friends. They taught me some great old dances, and they help me earn money by paying me to help in the yard and walk their dog, Fancy.

MR. AND MRS GOMEZ

RANDI lives in Florida. She's in the same grade I am. She loves snorkeling, playing volleyball, and eating hot dogs. She and her brother, Mason, live in a house near the motel where my family is staying in Florida.

RANDI

MASON is Randi's big brother. He's in eighth grade. He's really nice! He loves watching movies and playing dominoes. He told me that his favorite food is hamburgers. We have a lot of fun together!

MASON

INTRODUCTION

If it weren't for my friends, I'd be:

1. Bored

2. Lonely

3. Unhappy

Because of my friends, I:

1. Laugh a lot

2. Feel happy

3. Try new things

4. Have different experiences

In this book, you'll learn all about friends. Of course, there's no one right way to have a friendship. Friendships are as different as the people in them. Some of these tips and tricks might work for you. Others might not.

You know your friends best — you're the one who can best figure out how to be a GREAT FRIEND.

▷ CHAPTER 1
BE A BFF:
What it means to be a friend

My friends are the *most important people* in my life (besides my family).

I have three B**EST** friends: Monica, Becca, and Adam. We also hang out with Tommy and Peter. The six of us love doing things together, whether it's having a pool party, going to the mall, or just getting together to study.

I'm not a *popular princess*, but I get along with almost everyone. I'm not a snob about my friends. I don't care if they have cool clothes or a lot of money. But I do have some rules about what kind of friends I want to have.

I don't like having friends who aren't good listeners. I try to be a **good listener** to my friends, so I need friends who will listen to me.

I also like having friends who are FUNNY. Being able to make me smile when I'm feeling down? That's a great talent to have!

But I think the most important quality I look for in a friend is **kindness**. I don't want any friends who are mean or cruel.

Some people are nice to their friends, but MEAN or RUDE to other people — that's not okay with me. My friends are kind to everyone.

We don't have to like everyone, but if you ask me, we should try be nice to everyone.

Even **Anna Dunlap**.

Even JENNY PINSKI.

Even NICK WRIGHT.

It's hard to be nice to people sometimes, but it's worth it. And to me, it's the most important quality of a good friend.

Everybody knows that FRIENDS and *enemies* can make middle school good or bad. Luckily for me, my friends make everything in my life **GREAT!** They make it so great, in fact, that the people in my life who aren't my friends don't bother me at all.

There are as many kinds of friends as there are people, but there are a few common ways to split them up. Here are some of them. Think about your friends. Which category does each friend fit into?

Best friends

Some people think that you can only have one best friend. I know that's not true, since I have **three** best friends.

Best friends are the people who know everything about you. You feel very comfortable around your best friends. You love spending time with them. You can **trust** them with your secrets, and they trust you with theirs.

When something happens to you — whether it's something good or something bad — your best friends are the first people you tell. **BEST FRIENDS STICK BY YOU NO MATTER WHAT.**

Close friends

What's the difference between close friends and best friends? It's hard to explain.

I think of Tommy and Peter as being **MY CLOSE FRIENDS, BUT NOT BEST FRIENDS.** They don't know all of my secrets, but I do feel really comfortable with them.

They wouldn't be the first person I called if something FANTASTIC happened, but they'd find out my good news soon.

Friends

I have a lot of friends. They're not as close to me as my close friends and best friends, but I LOVE hanging out with them. Most people I know fit into this category.

Acquaintances

Acquaintances are people you know, but you don't know well. **You don't share secrets**. You don't call them when you're having a bad day. You SMILE at them in the hallway at school, but you don't walk home from school together.

An acquaintance might be someone in one of your classes, or another member of your basketball team. Everyone has lots of acquaintances.

Take this quiz to find out if you're a good friend.

1. At lunch, you spot a friend crying. What do you do?

a. Go over to talk to her and find out what's wrong.

b. Get in line to get your food. Maybe you'll talk to her after you're done eating, if there's time.

c. Ignore her. Crying in public is totally EMBARRASSING.

2. Your friend tells you that she **really likes** a certain boy and asks you not to tell anyone. **You:**

a. Keep the secret as long as you live.

b. Tell another friend, but ask them not to tell anyone.

c. Tell *everyone* right away — including the boy your friend likes.

3. You're having a birthday party. Who do you invite?

a. Your *best* friends.

b. EVERYONE in school.

c. Just the most **popular** girls.

4. Your friend is having a hard time with her English homework. What do you do?

a. Offer to help her study after school.

b. Give her your notes.

c. *Nothing*. You have your own homework, after all.

GOOD VS. EVIL

Is your friend a good or a bad friend? Here are some foolproof ways to tell.

Signs of a bad friend

- Does things on purpose to **HURT** your feelings

- Insults you

- Makes fun of you

- Doesn't keep secrets

- Talks about you **behind your back**

- Doesn't listen to your problems

- Only talks about himself or herself

- Doesn't **EVER** want to do things you want to do

- Doesn't want to help you

- Chooses to only spend time with others

- Doesn't understand you

- **DOESN'T CARE** about things going on in your life

Signs of a good friend

- Careful to not hurt your feelings

- Says things to make you feel good about yourself

- COMPLIMENTS you

- Keeps secrets that you tell her and him

- **Sticks up for you**

- Listens to you

- Is interested in what you have to say

- Tries to make you feel better when you're sad or upset

- Is *happy* when you're happy

- Understands you

- Chooses to spend time with you

- Wants to help you

- **CARES ABOUT YOU**

▷ CHAPTER 2
FRIENDSHIP FEATURES:
Keeping secrets & giving support

Spot the **true friendship!** Do you know when friendships are true? How do real friends treat each other? Which duo has the true friendship?

1. **Ava** and LILLY have been friends since kindergarten. Lilly loves shopping. Ava loves hiking. They spend most of their time at the mall. Ava sometimes wished she could hit the trails more. But she likes spending time with Lilly.

2. *Brooke* confided in **Tori** and told her that she was getting a D in science. Tori told another friend, who swore she wouldn't tell. But soon the whole class knew. So Brooke told Logan that Tori had a big crush on him.

3. **Mandy** and ZACH love video games. When they play, the loser has to buy the winner ice cream. Mandy is great at driving games. Zach is better at sports games. They both want to win, but they give each other tips to help the other improve.

So which is the true friendship? Lilly is a good friend to Ava, but the friendship seems a little ONE-SIDED. If two friends have different interests, they should take turns choosing what to do.

What about Tori and Brooke? It is pretty obvious that they aren't acting like real friends. Secret-keeping is one of the most important parts of friendship. Both of them have *loose lips*, and their friendship will suffer.

Mandy and Zach get it right. They have fun together and find ways to support one another. **BEING SUPPORTIVE IS WHAT FRIENDSHIPS ARE ALL ABOUT.**

No two friendships are exactly alike. But most friendships share some common features. These are the things that friends do for each other. **Friends . . .**

. . . keep secrets.

. . . support each other.

. . . do nice things for each other.

. . . know when to ask each other for help.

DON'T TELL ANYONE!

The **number-one rule** of middle school friendship is that if a friend tells you a secret, you can't tell anyone else. Even if it's a really good secret.

For example, Monica and Becca both know that I have a HUGE CRUSH on Brad Turino, our school's football star and one of the nicest guys in the seventh grade. But Brad doesn't know. And Brad doesn't know because my friends would never tell **ANYONE**. (Maybe eventually I'll tell Brad . . . but not yet!)

Monica and I know that Becca has a crush on Tommy, but we'd never tell anyone else. That's because we're best friends, and that's what good friends do — *keep secrets*.

Think of it this way: if you told your friend a secret, would you want him or her to tell anyone?

NO.

So you shouldn't tell anyone about your friend's secrets either. End of story. RIGHT?

Well, no. Not all secrets should be kept. What should you do if a friend has a secret that could hurt her? What if the secret is that someone is being mean to her, or hurting her, or doing something wrong?

That's a tough one. **But the truth is, you should help your friend.**

Sometimes helping a friend means keeping a secret. Sometimes helping your friend means telling the secret to someone else who can help your friend.

You know in your heart what the right thing to do is.

In that case, you're not breaking the rules of friendship. You're taking care of your friend. **THAT'S THE REAL NUMBER-ONE RULE OF FRIENDSHIP.**

If you decide that your friend's secret needs to be shared with someone who can help her, your friend might get upset.

Try to not take it personally. You know you did the right thing. And your friend will understand that too.

Another rule of being a good friend is supporting your friend when he or she is going through something difficult.

You count on your friends to help you when your life feels hard. If something goes **WRONG**, you turn to your friends for support. And in turn, you need to be supportive to your friends.

Sometimes that's not easy. It can be hard to help people.

For example, when Monica's grandma died two years ago, I wasn't sure what to say to help Monica. She was *so sad*. She cried a lot and didn't really want to do anything.

Becca and I wanted to make her happy, but we didn't know how.

Finally, I realized that Monica really **MISSED HER GRANDMA**. So we had a little memorial service in my tree house. Monica brought some pictures of her grandma and told us stories about her.

All Becca and I had to do was listen. Monica loved it, and she said it made her feel **a lot better** to share memories of her grandma with her best friends. Becca and I liked it too, because it was nice to see Monica feel better.

Another time, Becca suddenly started acting sad a lot. Monica and I kept asking her what was wrong, but she wouldn't tell us.

Eventually she admitted that she was getting *a bad grade in math* and wasn't sure how to fix it. She was having a really hard time with fractions.

Monica and I bought a frozen pizza, a chocolate cake, and a big jug of milk. We used those things to demonstrate fractions, and we had a DELICIOUS study session with Becca.

Soon, her grade started to go up!

Sometimes there's nothing you can do to make your friend feel better. That's okay. **Just listening is enough to be a great friend.**

GIVING SUPPORT

With these tips, you'll be a great source of support for your friends.

1. **DON'T NAG.** If you don't know what's wrong, don't push. Let your friend tell you when she is ready.

2. **WHEN YOUR FRIEND IS READY TO TALK TO YOU, LISTEN FIRST.** Don't ask a lot of questions until your friend is done talking.

3. **ASK QUESTIONS THAT WILL GET YOUR FRIEND TO TALK MORE.** Don't ask questions that can only be answered with "Yes", "No", or "Maybe."

4. **FIND OUT WHAT YOUR FRIEND NEEDS FROM YOU.** Does she want help with her problem? Does she just want someone to talk to? If she just wants someone to listen to her, but you try to fix her problem right away, it might make her feel worse.

5. **REMIND HER THAT YOU CARE** about her and that you want to help.

Death/sickness of a loved one

Let your friend talk. Don't try to talk about your own experiences unless your friend asks. Be a good listener.

Bad self esteem

If your friend is down on herself, remind her about how great she is. Tell her five things about herself that are wonderful.

Parents fighting

Let your friend know she is always welcome at your house. And be a good listener.

Sibling rivalry

Talk about your own problems with siblings (if you have any) to show her that she's not alone.

Bad grades

Offer to help with homework or studying. Set up a study group that includes your friend. Make plans to get together to work on schoolwork (and make it fun by having snacks, taking breaks, and helping each other when possible).

Disappointments (Not making the team/doing badly in a game/not getting the part she wanted in a play/etc.) Remind your friend of the reasons you like her. Tell her about things that you know she's good at.

Romantic trouble

Problems with boys can be really complicated. In this situation, what your friend needs most is a person to listen to her. A great thing to do with a friend who's having relationship issues (or almost any problem at all) is rent a funny movie, make some popcorn, and have a girls' night!

Fight with a friend

This can be a tricky one. If your friend is having a fight with another friend, you don't want to get in the middle (especially if you're friends with the other person). So how can you be supportive and still stay neutral (that's a fancy word for not picking a side)? Just listen to your friend. Offer advice if you have any. Don't say anything mean about the other person; just try to help your friend figure out a way to end the fight.

Sickness/injury

If your friend is sick or hurt, she probably can't do as much as she'd like to. You can be supportive by helping her out — bring her soup and DVDs, or help her by collecting her homework from teachers at school and bringing it to her house. Ask your friend what you can do to help.

What about other problems? **Think about what you'd want your friends to do, and do that.** You are the **BEST JUDGE** of how to be a good friend.

GETTING SUPPORT

You're a GREAT friend, right? And you have great friends. So how come sometimes you feel like no one cares about you?

Once I decided to have a big party and invite everyone in the seventh grade. It was a lot of work, and I was having a *really hard time* putting it all together.

I wanted to surprise my friends with the party. But because I was so busy, I wasn't being a very good friend.

I forgot about plans we'd made, and I didn't take any time to talk to my friends.

Pretty soon, they were MAD, and I still really needed help.

Luckily, once I told my friends what was up, they were there for me. It was the **best party ever** — and it proved that I have the best friends ever.

Here's what to do when YOU'RE the one with a problem.

- DON'T take it out on your friends. If you're having a hard time, it's easy to put on a tough face for the rest of the world but be mean or snippy to your friends.

- DO tell your friends about what's bothering you. They might be able to help, and it always helps to have someone to talk to.

- DON'T be afraid to ask for help. Your friends aren't mind-readers, after all!

- DO be patient. Your friends might not be able to help right away.

- DON'T be frustrated if your friends can't fix your problems. As long as they're listening to you, they're doing their jobs.

- DO be grateful you have such awesome friends!

❀ Honesty

I never want to hurt my friends' feelings. I would never tell Becca that her latest painting is UGLY, and I'd never tell Monica that sometimes she looks silly on her horse during riding lessons. (Neither of those things is true!)

But it's important to be honest with your friends. Don't lie to them. That doesn't mean you should tell your best friend that her new shirt is BORING. It means that if you have an opinion about something, even if it's different from your friend's opinion, you should feel comfortable telling them about it. It's okay to have your **own** ideas about things, after all.

Friends should be able to talk about their opinions. When two people can talk about their different opinions without getting angry, that's a sign of a good, strong friendship.

❀ Kindness

One of the *most important* things I look for in a friend is kindness. I don't want mean friends. Some people think mean people are funny — not me. I want friends who are nice to other people. My friends and I aren't perfect, but we're DEFINITELY all nice.

YOU CAN TELL IF SOMEONE IS NICE IF HE/SHE:

- **helps** other people
- doesn't spread RUMORS
- *smiles* at unpopular kids
- doesn't tell **JOKES** about other people
- STICKS up for his or her friends

❀ Sharing

Good friends share with each other. Becca, Monica, and I share clothes, DVDs, lunches, hair accessories, makeup . . . I don't think I have anything that I wouldn't share with them. And they trust me with their things too.

PRESENTS FOR FRIENDS

It can be hard to think of perfect presents for your friends. *Here are some ideas.*

FOR YOUR FRIEND WHO _____ A GREAT PRESENT IS _____

LOVES ART → A sketchbook and some colored pencils

LOVES MUSIC → A gift card for downloading MP3s

LOVES BEING OUTSIDE → A stainless steel water bottle

LOVES ANIMALS → A donation to the animal shelter in his or her name

LOVES COOKING → A box of fancy cookies

LOVES COMICS → A graphic novel

LOVES SPORTS → Tickets to a game

LOVES VIDEO GAMES → A t-shirt with his or her favorite game character

LOVES READING → A collection of short stories or poems

Treat Your Friend to Something Nice

Does your friend need **cheering up?** Here are some ways to make your friend happy.

- Buy her a few FLOWERS (yellow roses are traditional for friendship)

- Help her with her *homework*

- Trade your **DELICIOUS** grilled cheese for her **BORING** PB&J

- Go to her basketball game, and bring a sign cheering her on

- Invite her over for **ice cream** and *movies*

- Make a plan to meet up at the mall

- Go on a **PHOTO-HUNT WALK** and take pictures of cool things that you see together

- Get together to read magazines, and make a collage of your favorite images

▷ CHAPTER 3
FRIENDS WANTED:
How to reach out & make new friends

Every kid has to make new friends once in a while.
Here's how.

SEEK OUT PEOPLE WITH SIMILAR INTERESTS.

It's not a guarantee that every kid who likes
rollerblading as much as I do will be a good
friend, but at least it would give us something to talk
about. So if I needed to make a new friend, I'd look for
the kids who rollerblade after school.

THINK ABOUT THE WAYS YOU LIKE TO SPEND YOUR TIME.

Do you like reading? Check out the library. Look
for kids who are reading the kinds of books you like.

Are you more into drawing or painting? See if
anyone hangs out in the art room between classes
or at lunch.

If you love basketball, find the courts and ask to
join a game.

IF IT'S HARD TO FIND KIDS WHO HAVE THE SAME INTERESTS AS YOU, TRY JOINING A TEAM OR A CLUB AT SCHOOL.

Not only will you have something in common with the kids you'll meet, but you'll also be guaranteed to spend some time together.

Spending time together means you'll feel more comfortable, so you'll be yourself. And being yourself makes you likeable!

IF YOU DON'T WANT TO JOIN A CLUB OR A TEAM, TRY BEING BRAVE.

Find a table of interesting-looking kids and ask if you can sit with them at lunch. Or smile at a new person in the hallway and say hello.

Don't feel bad if the first person you talk to doesn't respond. It might take a while before you find the perfect people for you.

It's hard to make friends, so be proud of yourself for trying!

FROM ACQUAINTANCE TO FRIEND

Once you've made some ACQUAINTANCES, it's time to turn them into friends.

An easy way to do that is to ask someone to do something with you one-on-one.

Invite the person over for dinner, or ask if they'd like to go to the mall with you on the weekend. You'll be friends in *no time!*

Of course, not every acquaintance becomes a friend. That's okay. After all, you're two different people, and not all people get along. If that happens, don't be **EMBARRASSED** or sad. Just keep trying.

But don't stress about it. Friendships need to develop **naturally**. If you're too worried about it, it won't happen.

So you've read over my tips for making friends, and you think to yourself, **"Those are great tips, but I'm too shy."**

It usually doesn't bother me to talk to someone I don't know. I figure we will either hit it off, or we won't. NO BIGGIE. But I know that if you are shy, it is *really* hard to put yourself out there. Here are a few tips to help you.

REMEMBER THAT YOU ARE NOT ALONE. Lots of kids are shy. Grown-ups too. In fact, an Internet search for "tips on beating shyness" brings up almost 150,000 hits! If you talk to someone new, there is a good chance that they are shy too. Maybe they will be grateful to you for putting them at ease.

Pick out at least one outfit that you feel great in. Wear it when you know you'll be meeting new people. I always feel a little better when I have on a great outfit and my hair is fixed. I even feel a little braver. Talking to someone new is a lot easier if you feel confident.

☼ *Think of some ways to start a conversation.*
Pretend you are going to a club meeting for the first time. You can ask the person next to you if they are already a member or joining like you. You can also ask how they got interested in the club. Take a little time to think of questions, and remember that people like talking about themselves.

☼ **REMEMBER THAT NO ONE IS THINKING ABOUT WHAT YOU SAY AS MUCH AS YOU ARE.** That means that even if you think you have said the stupidest thing ever, the person you are talking to probably doesn't think so. If you are nice and friendly, people will want to talk with you. And if they don't, they are not worth your time anyway.

☼ **Talk to an adult about it.** Your teacher might be able to pair you up with an understanding and outgoing student. Your parents might have ideas about places you can practice meeting people.

Believe in yourself! You can OVERCOME YOUR SHYNESS. And once you do, you will be on your way to making new friends.

▷ CHAPTER 4
FRIENDSHIPS GONE WRONG:
How to fight fair

I've **NEVER** heard of two friends who don't sometimes have a fight. Even the best of friends sometimes have an argument.

Having an argument doesn't mean that a friendship needs to end or that there's something wrong with either of you. It just means that something in your friendship needs to be worked out.

Hurt feelings are probably the number-one reason good friends fight. **HERE'S HOW IT HAPPENS:**

1. **Friend 1**: Says something mean or hurtful (usually by accident).

2. **Friend 2:** Feels hurt and says something mean or hurtful back.

3. **Friend 1:** Also feels hurt and continues to say mean or hurtful things.

4. Then it keeps going.

Usually, the person who hurt the other person's feelings didn't mean to — after all, most people don't want to hurt their friends on purpose. (If your friend did hurt your feelings on purpose, he or she is not a very good friend!) But once a fight has started, that doesn't really matter.

To make sure this doesn't happen to you, stop and solve the problem before it turns into a fight. Like this:

1. **Friend 1:** Says something mean or hurtful (by accident).

2. **Friend 2:** "That hurt my feelings. I don't think you meant to hurt my feelings. What did you mean?"

3. **Friend 1:** Explains what he or she really meant.

4. Friends are happy and continue on.

See? No fight!

Fighting is normal, but that doesn't mean it's any fun. Luckily, it can usually be avoided. **Here's how.**

Be honest.

If a friend does something that upsets you, let your friend know. You don't have to react ANGRILY. You can calmly tell your friend what he or she did to upset you.

Try to use words that explain how you feel. Did your friend's actions make you feel sad, mad, confused? Tell him or her that. Your friend probably didn't mean to upset you. (If he or she did mean to upset you, that's a sign of a bad friend.)

Be brave.

Don't be afraid to tell your friend when you're upset. Ignoring a problem could make it even worse.

Be understanding.

If you know your friend didn't mean to hurt your feelings, think about what he or she might have meant before you react.

Be patient.

You might need to wait a few minutes — or a few days — before an argument is solved. That's okay, as long as you **keep thinking positive.**

Keep being a good friend, even though you're in a fight. Follow the rules of good friendship, and you'll see, everything will work out!

Sometimes, even though you try everything, a fight might continue. Once Monica and I were in an argument and we didn't speak to each other for three whole days!

It was HORRIBLE. I felt sick to my stomach the whole time.

Luckily, we worked it out. It turned out that we both needed a little time to cool off. Once we had a few days to think about it, we both realized that we wanted to save our friendship.

I called her to apologize, and she answered on the first ring. She had been just about to call me to apologize!

• **Take turns talking.** That way you each get to say what you need to say.

• **TRY NOT TO BRING UP OTHER FIGHTS.** Focus on the problem that's going on now.

• **Don't get your other friends involved.** If the fight is between you and one other person, it's not fair to your other friends to ask them to choose sides.

• **KEEP ACTING LIKE A GOOD FRIEND.** A fight doesn't mean that you should start being a bad friend.

• **Try to focus on other things.** Keep doing your homework, going to school, and enjoying yourself. Don't stop eating or going to school, even if you're really sad and upset. That won't help.

If your fight can't be resolved, don't be afraid to *ask for help*. A counselor at school, a teacher, a parent, or another friend could help by sitting down with you and your friend and helping you talk through the problem.

SAYING GOODBYE TO A FRIENDSHIP

Most fights can be solved. But once in a while, friendships do end. It's VERY SAD when they do. You should try to save your friendships, but it's not always possible.

If your friendship can't be saved, even though you've tried hard, it's okay to accept that and move on.

If you can, **end the friendship on good terms.** That means not saying bad things about the other person behind his or her back. Don't try to ruin his or her other friendships.

You should still be polite to your old friend. Who knows? Maybe you'll be friends again later.

It's hard to say goodbye to a friend. Remember that it's okay to be sad. Be kind to yourself. Tell your parents and friends about what happened so that they can comfort you. But don't stay sad for long. There are LOTS more friends out there just waiting to be made!

FEELING LEFT OUT

Becca and I are both in choir. During our practices, we have A LOT of fun. Our director is always making jokes, and at the end of practice, people take turns doing tricks.

Before a concert or competition, we have extra practices. Becca and I always end up talking about the funny things that happen in practice.

A few days before our last concert, I noticed Monica was acting kind of **weird**. She was sort of down and didn't talk much.

I asked her what was wrong, but she just kept saying she was fine. The day after our concert, she finally admitted that she had been feeling LEFT OUT. She couldn't laugh along with us when we talked about funny things that happened in choir, because she hadn't been there.

Becca and I didn't mean to leave Monica out. We both felt REALLY bad that she had felt bad. Now we make an effort to explain what happened in choir and talk about other things when we are with Monica.

What to do if you feel left out:

TALK TO YOUR FRIENDS. They probably don't realize that you feel left out. They are your friends. They would never leave you out on purpose.

TRY TO GET INVOLVED. Monica doesn't sing, so she would not enjoy choir. But she does try to stay involved with what we are doing. How? She comes to our concerts and competitions to cheer us on.

PLAN SPECIAL TIME TOGETHER. Becca and I were spending lots of extra time together. Monica wanted more time with us. A trip to the movies or the mall would have made her feel more included.

DISTRACT YOURSELF. If your friends are busy preparing for something like a competition, they should be more available after it is over. In the meantime, you need to keep busy and distract yourself. Learn a new hobby or spend some time volunteering. Local nursing homes and animal shelters are always looking for volunteers.

WHEN A FRIEND MOVES

I'm lucky — none of my friends have ever moved away. But when my brother, Jimmy, was my age, he wasn't so lucky. His best friend, Greg, moved to California.

Jimmy and Greg met in kindergarten. They became best friends. Greg lived pretty close to us, so every day, they would play together after school.

During summer vacations, they spent all of their time together. They were on the same **LITTLE LEAGUE** team. When they started middle school, they made sure that they had the same schedule.

But then, during the summer after sixth grade, Jimmy came home really UPSET one day after being at Greg's house. My mom asked what was bothering him, and we found out that Greg's mom had gotten a new job. The whole family was moving to California.

At first, Jimmy thought that meant his friendship with Greg was over. But he was wrong!

Now it's three years later. He and Greg are still friends. They aren't best friends anymore, but they're REALLY close.

Jimmy has gone to California to visit Greg, and Greg has come here to visit us.

They email, IM, and text each other all the time. They send each other birthday presents. They even play video games together over the Internet.

Jimmy says it's almost like Greg never left, except that they don't eat lunch together anymore.

I would be really sad if one of my best friends moved away. But according to my big brother, the friendship can be just as good after someone moves!

IT JUST TAKES SOME WORK TO KEEP A FRIENDSHIP STRONG WHEN YOU'RE NOT IN THE SAME TOWN. If you're committed to your friendship, distance shouldn't matter. You just need to make an effort to stay in touch, keep **UP-TO-DATE** on each other's lives, and try to do nice things for each other once in a while.

▷ CHAPTER 5
DARING DIVERSITY:
Being friends with someone different

My best friends are my age, and they are in the same grade as me at the same school. We have a lot in common. But you don't have to have EVERYTHING in common with someone in order to be friends with them.

In fact, I think that some of the best and most interesting friendships are with people who **AREN'T** exactly like me.

I love it that Becca and Monica are a lot like me. But I also love the things about them that aren't like me. For example, Monica is really brave about trying new things. And Becca is amazing at art. She has a ton of creative ideas.

But I really like my friends who don't have much in common with me at all.

> *They teach me about different things and help me see the world through different eyes.*

It's good to be friends with lots of different kinds of people — girls, boys, people from different backgrounds, people of different ages.

That's part of what makes having friends so fun. It wouldn't be fun if your friends were all exactly like you, right?

It would get REALLY BORING, REALLY FAST. And nobody wants to be bored by their friends.

My mom says that when she was my age, **NOBODY** had a computer. They hadn't even invented cell phones yet, and to send a message to a friend who didn't live in the same town, they had to write letters.

Nowadays, we have lots of ways to keep in touch with friends. I even have a few friends who I met online. In fact, we've **NEVER** even met in real life! (I'm always careful, though — see my safety tips on the next page.)

Here's how we keep in touch:

- We send lots of **emails**.

- I read their **blogs**, and they read mine (when I have time to update it!).

- We send each other **text messages** (when my dad lets me use his cell phone).

- We send each other **e-cards**, funny jokes, and cool **photos of celebrities**.

STAY SAFE ONLINE

- **Never use your full name.**

- **NEVER** give out your address or your phone number.

- If you use a social networking site (like Facebook or MySpace), be sure your profile is *private.* Only people you know should get to read your information or see your photos.

- **Never meet someone** you've met online without an adult. It is easy to lie about who you are online. You might think you are meeting a 14-year-old girl and end up meeting someone entirely different. (Think **CREEPY** old guy.)

- When you use a screen name, make sure it doesn't say much about you. If you include things like your name, age, hometown, or school, people are more likely to figure out who you are.

- **IF YOU'RE BEING TEASED ONLINE, TELL SOMEONE** you trust. Bullying is never okay, even on the computer.

Friends don't have to be in the same grade as you. In fact, they don't even have to be near your age! Some of my friends are older than me.

Mr. and Mrs. Gomez live across the street. They've been married for 45 years! And they were older than I am when they got married, so that means they're *really old!* They even have grandchildren.

Even though they're not my age, we get along really well. Mrs. Gomez taught me COOL old dances for a school dance. Every day after school, I would go over and hang out with her for an hour or two.

Her husband, Mr. Gomez, gives me advice about things all the time. He also pays me to help him take care of his lawn and clean up after Mrs. Gomez's dog, Fancy. When I needed to earn more money, he recommended me to one of our neighbors. Then she hired me to do some work for her.

The Gomezes are great. They're like friends and grandparents rolled into one!

IT'S NICE TO HAVE OLDER FRIENDS. HERE'S WHY:

- I don't see them every day at school, so I can get a fresh take on things I tell them. They can give me an **honest answer.**

- They used to be kids. So they can give me a GROWN-UP'S PERSPECTIVE, but they remember what it was like to be a kid.

- They have had lots of **different experiences.** They remember whole decades I wasn't even alive in! That comes in handy for history homework, but it also helps to hear about things that happened before I was born from people who actually experienced them.

- They're always willing to LISTEN.

- They like having a *connection* to younger people. Mr. and Mrs. Gomez's grandchildren don't live close, so they treat me kind of like a grandkid. My grandma lives near me, but I don't mind having a special relationship with Mr. and Mrs. Gomez too!

YOUNGER FRIENDS

Just like you can have friends who are older, you can also have friends who are younger. I would NOT call **Nick Wright** my friend. He's the bratty seven-year-old who lives next door to me. I get stuck babysitting him all the time when his mom has other things she has to do. Sometimes I don't even get paid, because my mom says that we should do nice things for our neighbors.

Nick's not my friend. But I have to admit that sometimes, I enjoy hanging out with him. I don't have any younger brothers or sisters. I do have younger cousins, but I don't see them that often. So sometimes, it's kind of fun to hang out with Nick. We can play with toys that my friends think they're too old for. I can still scare him with **ghost stories**, and we watch cartoons together.

OH NO. I think I just realized that NICK WRIGHT is kind of my friend!

When I was little, I met a girl at school named NATALIE. One day, I invited her over to my house. She said she couldn't come over because my family was different from her family.

I was a little kid, so I didn't really understand what she was saying. But now I do, and it makes me **angry**. Even though I didn't really get it when I was younger, when Natalie said that to me, I decided I'd never choose my friends based on the ways they were the same as me.

It's nice to have the same hobbies, or similar tastes in movies or TV shows, but things like *religion*, skin *color*, or the amount of **MONEY** someone has won't stop me from being friends with them.

Natalie goes to a different school now. I hope she's changed her mind about what makes a good friend.

BOY FRIENDS, NOT BOYFRIENDS

Adam, one of my best friends of all time, is a boy. So are Peter and Tommy. I don't see any reason to not be friends with boys. I think it's kind of STRANGE that lots of girls stop being friends with boys once they're not little kids anymore.

Some girls only want to be friends with boys so that boys can do things they don't want to do, like get rid of **BUGS** or fix things. But I think girls can do **anything** boys can do.

I don't like **CREEPY CRAWLIES**, and I'm not CRAZY about getting dirty, but I know I can get rid of any bug and fix almost anything. I don't need a boy around to help me with that. But I like having friends who are boys.

Sometimes it gets AWKWARD. For example, I don't want to talk to Adam about my crush on Brad Turino. But that's not because I don't trust Adam, or because I don't like telling Adam about what's happening in my life.

It's because Brad is a friend of Adam's. They play sports together. And I would feel strange if Adam knew that I had a CRUSH on his friend. It would make me uncomfortable.

Adam also doesn't know that Becca has a crush on Tommy. But maybe he knows that Tommy has a crush on Becca! After all, he's really good friends with Tommy.

Anyway, there's no reason to stay away from your friends who are boys, or to try to not become friends with a boy. Boys do have different experiences than girls do. *That's okay.*

A note about boyfriends . . .

If you do have a **boyfriend**, remember he is not the only important thing in your life. Sometimes girls forget their friends when they have a crush. Your friends are always there for you. **GIVE THEM THE ATTENTION THEY DESERVE!**

PAL AROUND ON VACATION

Over winter break, I went to Florida with my family. My friends didn't come along, so I figured I'd be spending a lot of time by myself.

But I was lucky. One day, when I went down to the beach alone, I met two kids. RANDI and MASON lived near the motel where my family was staying.

Over the next few days, we hung out **all the time!** We went to the beach, played dominoes, watched movies, and went to a parade. My mom talked to Mason and Randi's mom before I spent a lot of time with them. It was so much fun. It changed a really boring vacation into the BEST VACATION EVER.

Mason and Randi and I are still friends. They're planning to visit me soon, and I'd love to go back to Florida to see them. We stay in touch by writing emails, sending text messages, and sometimes talking on the phone. For **special** occasions, I love sending them real mail. Once in a while, when Monica, Becca, and I make chocolate chip cookies (our specialty), I send some to my Florida friends.

How can you make friends when you're not at home? Vacations can be LAME when you're stuck hanging out with your family the whole time. **Here are some ways to make friends with kids your age while you're on vacation.**

- With your parents' permission, check out the places you'd hang out at home — **MALLS, LIBRARIES, MOVIE THEATERS, THE BEACH.**

- Keep an eye out in your hotel. *See anyone your age?* Talk to them next time you're at the pool or getting ice from the ice machine.

- If you're traveling as a group, at a resort, or on a cruise, sign up for kids' activities. (Good for two things: getting some time away from your family, and meeting new people.)

- Be FRIENDLY and OUTGOING (but stay safe!). Never go to someone's hotel room or house or anywhere alone without talking to your parents first.

▷ CHAPTER 6
THE UNFRIENDS:
Dealing with those who aren't so friendly

Just like friends are a huge part of every middle-schooler's COMPLICATED life, unfriends are too.

(Note: Unfriends are what other people might call enemies. I don't like that word — it seems too mean, as if you're in the middle of a **big, horrible war** with the other person or something. I like the word "unfriend," because it just means someone who is the opposite of a friend. I made up the word, but I like it anyway!)

Unfortunately, I don't get along with everybody. I really wish I did. It would be **so cool** to like everyone, and have everyone like me. But that's not the way the world works.

That's why I think everyone needs to learn about unfriends. *They are a fact of life.* Every person I know has at least one unfriend.

I just try to not think about them. I'd rather focus on my friends — not my unfriends.

When YOU are the unfriend

If someone doesn't like you, that's OKAY. It's hard to believe, but there isn't a single person in the world who's liked by everyone. **It's impossible!**

But what should you do if someone doesn't like you, even though you want them to?

1. **JUST KEEP BEING YOURSELF.** Anyone who doesn't like you isn't worth your time!

2. **CONTINUE TO BE CONSIDERATE** and thoughtful of others.

3. **MAKE SURE YOU'RE NOT SAYING ANYTHING HURTFUL —** even by accident. Being kind means not saying racist, sexist, or otherwise hateful things.

4. **DON'T WORRY ABOUT IT TOO MUCH.** Like I said, nobody is liked by everyone. (Even the popular kids.)

There are a few kinds of unfriends. Here's a guide so you can spot which kind you're dealing with . . . and figure out how to handle them.

Arch rival

Who it is: Someone you are really **COMPETITIVE** with. Maybe it's the other kid who's really good at math, or someone on your volleyball team, or a girl who likes the boy you like. It's never fun to have an arch rival, but they are sometimes a fact of middle school life.

How to deal: The best way to deal with an arch rival is to remind yourself of the ways that you're unique. You might not be the ONLY great math student, or the ONLY star setter, but you're unique and have your own talents.

Ex-friend

Who it is: A person you used to be close to. It happens to lots of friendships: two people are good friends, but then an argument that can't be resolved SPLITS them up.

How to deal: Be polite. No matter why you're not friends anymore, it's important to still be NICE. After all, your friendship might be fixable at some point.

Bully

Who it is: The person who TERRORIZES your whole school (or just you).

How to deal: There are a few different ways to handle a bully. Turn to page 67 for more.

Popular Princess

Who it is: The girl who's the most POPULAR one in the whole school. At my school, that's ANNA DUNLAP. She doesn't care about anyone except herself, and she's not nice at all. She teases everyone, she leaves people out, and she doesn't try to make anyone else happy. She's not even nice to her friends!

How to deal: Ignore her. Have fun with your friends — don't worry about what people like Anna Dunlap think.

Bullies are a fact of life in every middle school. At my school, the bully's name is **JENNY PINSKI**. She's taller than everyone else — even some of the teachers — and she's mean. Even Anna Dunlap is scared of Jenny.

Jenny has been TERRORIZING my grade since we were in kindergarten. You have to really watch your step around her — one wrong move and she'll get you.

Of course, even though she's been threatening to stomp us for eight years, I've never heard of anyone getting stomped. Then again, if Jenny Pinski stomped me, I wouldn't tell anyone . . . I would be too scared that she'd stomp me again for revenge!

Once, my worst **NIGHTMARE** came true: I had to work on a science project with Jenny. While we were partners, I was afraid to stand up to her. But once I did, I realized that Jenny wasn't a bully just to be mean. She was a bully whenever she thought someone was teasing HER. I still haven't relaxed around Jenny, but she's not as bad as I thought she was.

How to Deal with a Bully

What should you do if a bully bullies you? Here are some **tips and tricks** for dealing with your very own Jenny Pinski:

- **IGNORE THEM**. Bullies only have as much power as you give them.

- If the bully won't stop, **TALK TO AN ADULT ABOUT IT.** Don't be embarrassed to talk to a teacher or parent about the problem. It is your right to not be bullied.

- **DON'T BE AFRAID.** That can be hard, but if you're less afraid, a bully is less likely to continue to pick on you.

- **STAND UP TO THEM.** But don't bully back. There are already too many bullies in the world.

- **KEEP YOUR EYES OPEN.** If you see a bully bugging your friends, help your friends out. Walk over and stand next to your friend. Strength in numbers!

I don't really care about being popular, but I know some people do. At my school, *Anna Dunlap* is the **popular princess**. Even though she's mean and bossy, everyone wants to be like her and liked by her. Everyone does what she says. Except me. I don't put up with Anna.

Being popular isn't important to me. What's important to me is having good friends whom I trust. Some people would rather be popular than have REAL FRIENDS.

Luckily, my friends don't feel like that. Once, though, Monica decided she wanted to join the cheerleading squad. At my school, only the popular girls become cheerleaders. Monica knew that, and since she wanted to be a cheerleader, she decided to try to become popular.

But to get the popular girls to like her, Monica had to change. They made her do embarrassing things, like sing *"I'M A LITTLE TEAPOT"* at lunch. They didn't really like her. They just wanted to boss her around.

Monica realized that and decided it wasn't worth it. She would rather have her real friends than be a popular princess.

It was hard for me and Becca, though. WE FELT LIKE WE'D LOST OUR FRIEND! We wanted Monica to be happy, but it was hard to watch her hanging out with the popular girls instead of us.

If one of your friends suddenly becomes popular, what should you do?

First, see what happens. A good friend won't desert you just because she's popular.

Then focus on things you like about yourself and your friends. Maybe you don't have the most expensive clothes, or the newest, coolest video game system. What do you have that's *wonderful?* I bet you could make a really long list.

FINALLY, IF YOUR FRIEND DOESN'T TREAT YOU RIGHT, TALK TO HER. SHE MIGHT NOT HAVE REALIZED HOW SHE'S BEEN ACTING. REMEMBER TO BE CALM AND TELL HER HOW YOU FEEL.

▷ P.S.

They COMFORT you when you're sad. They help you when you're in trouble. They make you **happy** when you're down. They take care of you when you're SICK. Without friends, life would be pretty *boring*.

My friends are really important to me, and I know I'm important to them, too.

I hope this book about friends has helped you think about your own friendships. **If you're as lucky as I am, you have great friends.**

With great friends, you can do anything!

ABOUT THE AUTHOR

Diana G. Gallagher lives in Florida with her husband and five dogs, four cats, and a CRANKY parrot. Her hobbies are gardening, garage sales, and grandchildren. She has been an English equitation instructor, a professional folk musician, and an artist. However, she had aspirations to be a professional writer at the age of twelve. She has written *dozens of books* for kids and young adults.

ABOUT THE ILLUSTRATOR

Brann Garvey lives in Minneapolis, Minnesota, with his wife, Keegan, their dog, Lola, and their very fat cat, Iggy. Brann graduated from Iowa State University with **A BACHELOR OF FINE ARTS DEGREE**. He later attended the Minneapolis College of Art and Design, where he studied illustration. In his free time, Brann enjoys being with his family and friends. *He brings his sketchbook everywhere he goes.*

GLOSSARY

acquaintances (uh-KWAYN-tuhns-iz)—people you do not know very well

apologize (uh-POL-uh-jize)—to say that you are sorry about something

awkward (AWK-wurd)—difficult or uncomfortable

confident (KON-fuh-duhnt)—having a strong belief in yourself and your abilities

embarrassed (em-BARE-uhst)—felt uncomfortable

perspective (pur-SPEK-tiv)—a certain way of looking at something

resolved (ri-ZOLVD)—fixed a problem

supportive (suh-PORT-iv)—something that gives help and encouragement is supportive

terrorizing (TER-uh-rize-ing)—frightening someone a great deal

volunteering (vol-uhn-TEER-ing)—doing a job or service without pay

DISCUSSION QUESTIONS

1. Claudia has several rules she tries to follow when fighting with a friend. What rules do you think are **important** to follow during a fight?

2. What QUALITIES do you look for in a friend? How important is it to have things in common with your friend?

3. What do you like doing with your friends? Describe *a perfect day* with your best friends.

WRITING ACTIVITY

Pretend you are an **ADVICE COLUMNIST** for your favorite magazine. What advice would you give to solve these problems?

1. My friend Katie has a **new boyfriend**, Ben. She spends almost every spare minute with him! When she does manage to hang out with me, all she does is talk about Ben between sneaking him text messages. How can I tell her that this BUGS me?

2. My good friend thinks that things like *burping* really loud is hilarious. I think it is **gross and immature**. How can I get her to stop?

3. My friend's parents are getting a **DIVORCE**. I don't know what to say or do to make her feel better. Things feel WEIRD between us. What should I do?

STRAIGHT FROM TEENS

Here's what real teens, just like you, have to say about dealing with friends.

I thought my BFF and I were going to be friends forever. But one summer we stopped talking. It was hard. I didn't have any other really good friends. So I joined track and made a ton of new friends. Join new clubs or new sports to make new friends. After you get over the scary "I don't know anyone" part, it's fun!

—Brittany, 16

If you have an argument with a friend, it is really important to never say something that will really offend your friend. After all, a disagreement shouldn't lead to the loss of a friendship.

—Tamara, 17

READ UP
FOR MORE GREAT ADVICE!

☆ *The Girls' Guide to Friends: Straight Talk on Making Close Pals, Creating Lasting Ties, and Being an All-Around Great Friend* by Julie Taylor

☆ *For Girls Only: Wise Words, Good Advice* by Carol Weston

☆ *I've Got This Friend Who . . . Advice for Teens and Their Friends on Alcohol, Drugs, Eating Disorders, Risky Behaviors, and More* by America's teens and the experts at KidsPeace

☆ *Life Lists for Teens: Tips, Steps, Hints, and How-tos for Growing Up, Getting Along, Learning, and Having Fun* by Pamela Espeland

☆ *Mean Chicks, Cliques, and Dirty Tricks: A Real Girl's Guide to Getting Through the Day with Smarts and Style* by Erika V. Shearin Karres

CLAUDIA

CRISTINA CORTEZ

MORE FUN with Claudia!

When you're thirteen, like Claudia, life is complicated. Luckily, Claudia has lots of ways to cope with family, friends, school, work, and play. And she's sharing her advice with you! Read all of Claudia's advice books and uncomplicate your life.

CLAUDIA
CRISTINA CORTEZ
UNCOMPLICATES YOUR LIFE
Advice ABOUT SCHOOL
BY DIANA G. GALLAGHER

CLAUDIA
CRISTINA CORTEZ
UNCOMPLICATES YOUR LIFE
Advice ABOUT FAMILY
BY DIANA G. GALLAGHER

CLAUDIA
CRISTINA CORTEZ
UNCOMPLICATES YOUR LIFE
Advice ABOUT WORK AND PLAY
BY DIANA G. GALLAGHER

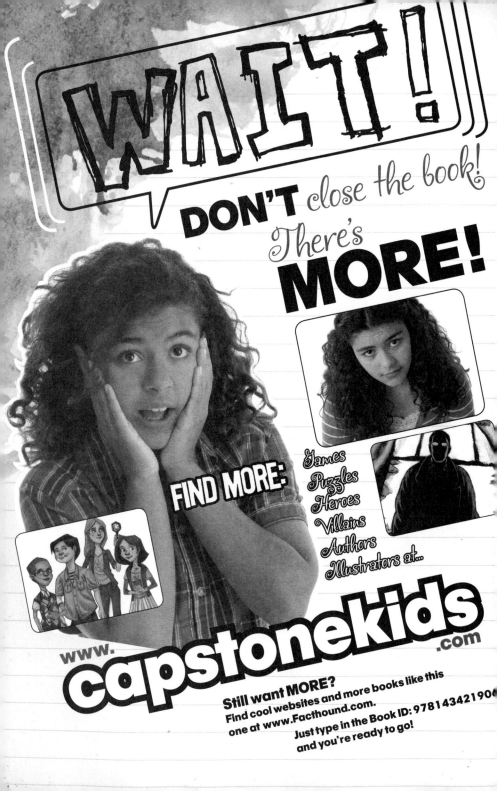